Monkey See, Monkey Do

A humorous
traditional story

First published in 2006 by
Franklin Watts
338 Euston Road
London
NW1 3BH

Franklin Watts Australia
Hachette Children's Books
Level 17/207 Kent Street
Sydney
NSW 2000

A CIP catalogue record for this book is available
from the British Library.

ISBN 0 7496 6550 5 (hbk)
ISBN 0 7496 6557 2 (pbk)

Series Editor: Jackie Hamley
Series Advisors: Dr Barrie Wade, Dr Hilary Minns
Design: Peter Scoulding

Printed in China

Monkey See, Monkey Do

Written by
Anne Adeney

Illustrated by
Christina Bretschneider

W
FRANKLIN WATTS
LONDON•SYDNEY

Anne Adeney

"Chattering monkeys sound just like people talking. But what do they talk about? Perhaps this story will give you a clue!"

Christina Bretschneider

"I have two cats. They like to sleep on my desk or play with my pencils. I think they're just as naughty as monkeys."

"Grandpa Mojo," said Sunny.
"You look like you're wearing a
giant rainbow banana!"

Sunny's grandpa was a pedlar
who sold coloured caps.

"The easiest way to carry the caps
is on my head!" laughed Mojo.

"Now I must be off to the forest villages to sell them."

The villages were far away and Mojo
walked for hours before stopping
to sleep.

Mojo woke up and looked around.

"Where are my caps?" he cried.

"Give me back my caps!" he roared,
and shook his fist.

Each monkey chattered at Mojo
and shook its fist.

11

"Give me back my caps!" he roared,
and stamped his feet.

Each monkey chattered at Mojo
and stamped its feet.

That gave Mojo a good idea.

"Monkey see, monkey do!"

he said to himself.

"Bad monkeys!" he roared, and
threw his own cap onto the ground.

15

Each monkey chattered at Mojo and
threw its cap onto the ground.
Mojo gathered up all the caps.

Then he put them back on his head
and went on his way. "What a story
I'll have to tell Sunny," he thought.

The years passed and old Mojo
stopped working.

Sunny was now a tall, young man.
He had always wanted to be a
pedlar like his grandpa.

The villages were far away
and Sunny walked for hours
before stopping to sleep.

Sunny woke up and looked around.

"Where are my caps?" he said.

"Give me back my caps!" he roared,
and shook his fist.

Each monkey chattered at Sunny and shook its fist.

"Give me back my caps!" he roared
and stamped his feet. Each monkey
chattered at Sunny and stamped
its feet.

Then Sunny remembered Grandpa Mojo's story. "Monkey see, monkey do!" he thought to himself.

"Bad monkeys!" he roared and threw
his own cap onto the ground.

The monkeys chattered back at
Sunny but they did not throw down
their caps.

"Whatever happened to 'monkey see, monkey do!' like my grandpa told me?" wailed Sunny.

A monkey jumped down, picked
up Sunny's hat and put it on her
baby's head.

"You silly man!" said the monkey.
"Monkeys have grandpas too,
you know!"

Notes for parents and teachers

READING CORNER has been structured to provide maximum support for new readers. The stories may be used by adults for sharing with young children. Primarily, however, the stories are designed for newly independent readers, whether they are reading these books in bed at night, or in the reading corner at school or in the library.

Starting to read alone can be a daunting prospect. READING CORNER helps by providing visual support and repeating words and phrases, while making reading enjoyable. These books will develop confidence in the new reader, and encourage a love of reading that will last a lifetime!

If you are reading this book with a child, here are a few tips:

1. Make reading fun! Choose a time to read when you and the child are relaxed and have time to share the story.

2. Encourage children to reread the story, and to retell the story in their own words, using the illustrations to remind them what has happened.

3. Give praise! Remember that small mistakes need not always be corrected.

READING CORNER covers three grades of early reading ability, with three levels at each grade. Each level has a certain number of words per story, indicated by the number of bars on the spine of the book, to allow you to choose the right book for a young reader:

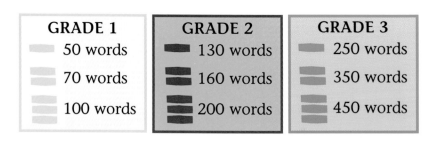

GRADE 1	GRADE 2	GRADE 3
50 words	130 words	250 words
70 words	160 words	350 words
100 words	200 words	450 words